This edition published by Parragon Books Ltd in 2014

Parragon Books Ltd
Chartist House
15–17 Trim Street
Bath BA1 1HA, UK
www.parragon.com

Written by Catherine Hapka
Illustrated by Grace Lee

ISBN 978-1-4723-5653-6

Printed in China

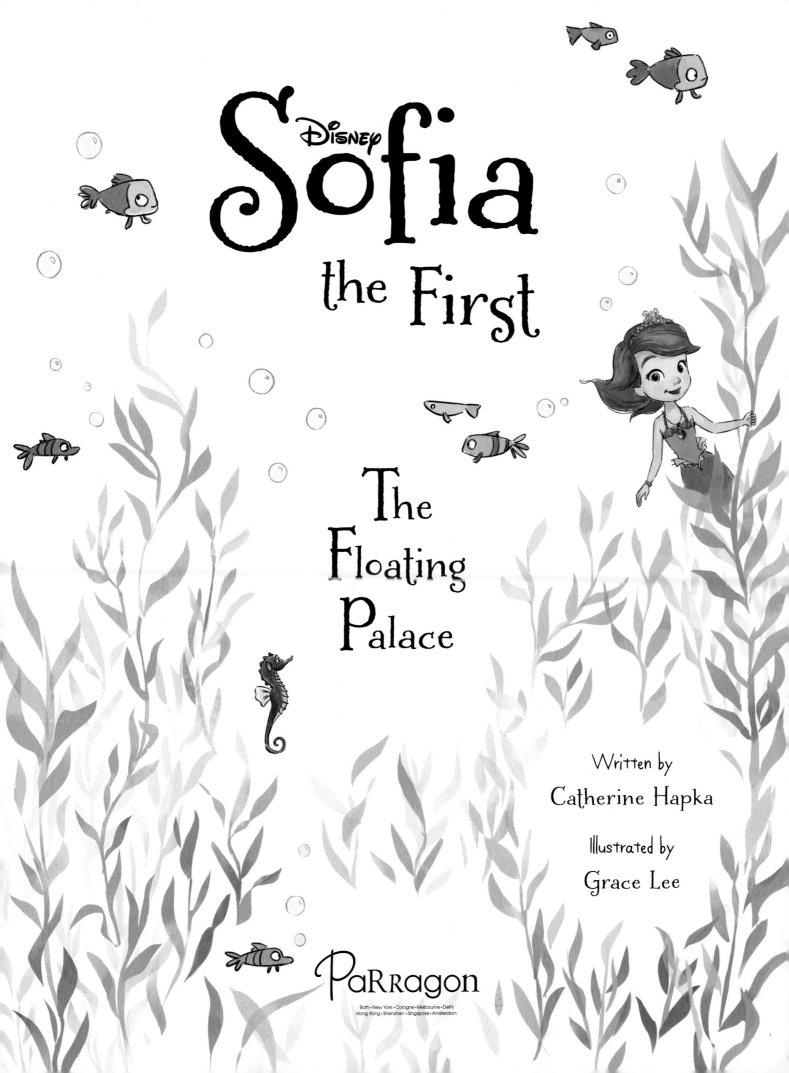

Disney
Sofia
the First

The Floating Palace

Written by

Catherine Hapka

Illustrated by

Grace Lee

PaRRagon

Bath · New York · Cologne · Melbourne · Delhi
Hong Kong · Shenzhen · Singapore · Amsterdam

I'm Sofia

and I love being a
princess.

For our summer holiday, my family
is visiting Merroway Cove on our boat.

It's so big, it's more
like a floating palace!

Lately, I've been reading about mermaids.
Maybe we'll see one at the cove. I hope so!
But Dad says mermaids aren't real.

My dad, King Roland, is usually right about most things – but he's wrong about mermaids.

Because when I go onto the deck of our floating palace, there she is – a real, live mermaid!

"Help!" the mermaid cries. Oh, no! She's tangled in a net!

"Let me help you," I say. I pull her onto
the boat and help to untangle her.
"Thank you!" she says. Her name is Oona.
She's really nice. Then she says she has to go.

"We're not supposed to spend time above the water,"
she explains. But when Oona gets in the water,
she can't swim. Her fin is hurt.

As I slide into the water to help her, my amulet glows - and I turn into a

mermaid!

I can't believe it!
And neither can Oona.
"How did you do that?" Oona asks.
I tell her about my **magical amulet**.
Oona has a comb that's enchanted, too.
"I'm not sure what its powers are,"
says Oona, "but Mum says she'll
tell me when I'm older."

I help Oona swim towards her home in the cove. We swim past a kelp forest, a cool sunken ship and hundreds of beautiful fish.

When we get near Oona's home, I meet
her friend, Sven the seahorse, and her big sister, Cora.
They use moon kelp to heal Oona's tail.

Suddenly, the water goes dark.
It's our **floating palace**
stopping above us.

Then we hear Oona's mum
calling her and Cora home.
Oona's mum is the
mermaid queen.

"I'm so glad you're safe!"
she says. "A human vessel
is in the cove and humans
are dangerous."

I'm not dangerous and neither
is my family. Queen Emmaline
doesn't know that, though.

She wants to use her magic trident to create a powerful storm – one that could blow the floating palace out of the cove, or maybe even **sink** it! My family is on that ship!

So I tell the queen that
I'm a human and I can get the ship to leave.
"Please don't sink it. Just give me a chance," I say.
Luckily, the queen agrees to let me try.
Oona and Cora wish me luck.

I start swimming back to the floating palace.
Suddenly, I hear Oona calling my name.

Oh, no! A horrible, hideous sea monster
is chasing her! He wants her enchanted comb.
I swim after them as fast as I can,
but then they enter the kelp forest.

"Oona!" I cry.
There's no answer.

I rush back and tell
Queen Emmaline what happened.
She says I have till sundown
to rescue Oona.
The queen says if I can't,
she'll sink the floating palace!

I swim back to
the floating palace.
I need help, but my family
doesn't believe
in mermaids.

So I gather some friends who
do believe – Sven, Clover
and a seagull named Farley.

Finally, we find Oona. The sea monster
has her trapped and he's about to steal her
enchanted comb. I try to stop him, but he's very
powerful – he almost captures me, too!

Oh, no!

Queen Emmaline is starting loud thunder over the cove!

I need to rescue Oona before her mum sinks my family's ship.

I don't know what to do....

"Sofia, your necklace
is glowing," Sven tells me.

When we dive underwater,
Princess Ariel appears!
My amulet brought her to help.
So I tell Ariel about Oona.
"I tried to save her, but...."
"You need more help," Ariel says.
She tells me that humans and
mermaids both love their families,
and if we just work together....

Now I know what to do!

Sven and I find
Cora and tell her
about the sea monster.

"He's after Oona's comb,"
I explain. "The only
way to save her is for
us to work together."

So Cora and
I come up with a plan.
Sven, Farley and Clover help, too.

I have to sneak onto the boat where the
sea monster has Oona trapped. I get there
just as he is about to cast a spell to grab
Oona's comb. I snatch it out of his hand!

"Give me the comb and I'll let your mermaid friend go," the sea monster says.

"What if I don't?" I say.

"Then I'll cast a spell on you and make you disappear!"

I step in front of Oona's cage.
Then I throw the comb
overboard, where Cora
is waiting to catch it.

"No you don't!"
the sea monster howls.
He flicks his wand at me ...

... but I quickly jump out
of the way. Instead of
making **me** disappear,
he makes Oona's cage vanish!

Oona is free! But the sea
monster is furious.
He points his wand at us.

"You won't trick me again!"
he warns.

Suddenly, Farley flies
over the sea monster –
and **drops** Clover right
on top of him!

Then Farley **swoops** down
and grabs his wand.

Cora holds up the comb
as it starts to glow!
"Waters, **rise** at my command!"
she cries. Then a spiral of water
blasts the sea monster
across the cove!

We rush back to Queen Emmaline.
"Thank goodness you're safe!" the queen cries.
She raises her trident to stop the storm.
Phew! Now my family is safe, too!

Oona's family and I go back to
the floating palace. We can't wait
for our two families to meet!
Dad admits he didn't think mermaids
were real, but now he knows!

I sit with Oona and watch the sun set.
She's a mermaid and I'm a human,
but I know
we'll be friends
forever!

The End